"You didn't bark at the thief?"

"Oh, no. Dogs get in trouble for barking and growling."

"You didn't bite him?"

"Heaven forbid! I never bite. *Never!*"

Red fell on his side. He rolled back and forth, and he laughed and laughed. Finally he got to his feet and started digging.

"Dogs shouldn't dig," I warned him. "You'll get in trouble."

"No, I won't," he said. "My master won't see the hole or the dirt."

"Please don't dig. I had a friend named Scotty. He was a digger. His master took him to the pound. And when you go to the pound . . . well, no one ever comes back from the . . . the *pound!*"

BILL WALLACE

WATCHDOG AND THE COYOTES

Illustrated by David Slonim

A MINSTREL® HARDCOVER
PUBLISHED BY POCKET BOOKS

New York   London   Toronto   Sydney   Tokyo   Singapore

A MINSTREL HARDCOVER

 A Minstrel Book published by
POCKET BOOKS, a division of Simon & Schuster Inc.
1230 Avenue of the Americas, New York, NY 10020

Text copyright © 1995 by Bill Wallace
Illustrations copyright © 1995 by David Slonim

Library of Congress Cataloging-in-Publication Data

ISBN: 0-671-53620-6

First Minstrel Books hardcover printing September 1995

10 9 8 7 6 5 4 3 2

A MINSTREL BOOK and colophon are registered trademarks of Simon & Schuster Inc.

Cover art by David Slonim

Printed in the U.S.A.

For
Kristine and Bethany Whitener

Chapter 1

*T*he warm dry breeze that swept in from the desert felt good on my cold nose. It tingled the little hairs inside my ears and made them twitch and wiggle. My left paw dangled over the edge of my floor. I draped my right paw over it and rested my chin.

I watched.

The sun was nothing but a huge orange sliver above the wooden fence around the backyard. It was pretty, but I forced myself to quit thinking about it. I had to watch. That was my job—and I couldn't afford to mess up again. This was my third chance—probably my last.

In a moment the sun would disappear and the

only thing left would be a bright glow. Higher in the sky were mixtures of yellow and gold. Streaks of clouds were darker. Low in the sky, they were blue. Above, the blue changed to a deep purple. I wished the fence wasn't there. I wished—just once—I could see all of the sunset.

Far off in the desert a coyote howled. It was a lonely sound. It made me feel lonely, too.

I watched.

But behind my eyes, visions came. Memories flooded my mind. I missed my mama. She had been so big and wise. I missed my little boy. He had been fun and full of laughter. I missed my big boy. He was rough-and-tumble, and I could play with him and not have to worry about him crying. How I longed to be with them.

Not that I didn't love my new master. He was nice. His laugh rolled and tumbled through the air like thunder rumbling before a storm. But he was just too old to play. His wife didn't play with me, either. They fed me well. They petted me and scratched behind my ears. But there was no romp or play in either of them. That was what made me lonely, especially on nights like this, when they weren't home.

I watched.

After a time, the deep purple color filled the

sky. The smell of night came and all was quiet, and the quiet made me feel even more alone.

Things could have been worse, I guess. That's why it was so important for me to watch. That's why I had to do a good job. I had to be careful.

Scotty had warned me. Scotty was a Scottie. He had lived in the yard next to mine back when I lived in California. There had been a chain-link fence between our houses, and not only could we visit but we could actually see each other. Scotty told me that he was a digger.

"It's a bad habit," he'd explained. "I just can't quit digging. It's kind of like some masters have a habit of smoking cigarettes, and no matter how hard they try, they just can't break the habit. I'm like that, too. Only I don't smoke, I dig."

Scotty was on his third master when I met him. Two days after our last visit Scotty dug up the guy's rosebushes, and sure enough—straight to the pound.

That's it, man. About three masters is all a guy gets, then off to the pound.

Despite the warm breeze from the desert, the memory of Scotty sent a chill up my back. The Shaffers were my third masters.

A sound jerked me from my sad memories. I watched.

For a time there was nothing. Then a black stocking cap appeared above the back fence. It hesitated there a moment, then rose. I watched.

A man's face was under the hat. Nervous eyes scanned my yard. A wisp of the fall breeze brought a scent to my nose. Something about it was almost familiar, but it was a smell I didn't know, an odor that I couldn't taste or understand. The man looked all around. Then there was another clunk as his shoe found the wood rail and he climbed over the fence.

I watched.

Wonder why he didn't use the gate, I thought as he jumped from the top of the fence. When he landed, he looked all around again. He had on a black cap and a black shirt and black pants. The only part I could really see of him was his face. His eyes and forehead scrunched up when he looked toward my doghouse. The way he acted, the way he smelled—it brought a feeling from deep inside me. His actions made the hair bristle in a sharp ridge down my back. He inched forward. Watching him made my lip curl. My teeth felt dry. He stood very still for a moment, then edged toward the house.

I watched.

I guess he hadn't seen me where I rested inside my house. When he got close he suddenly froze, dead in his tracks. He started to shake all over.

"Nice doggy." His voice quivered when he whispered to me. "Nice puppy."

The smell was much stronger now. I still couldn't hear or see or understand it. I forced my lips closed so my teeth wouldn't show. I made the hair relax on my back. My tail made a thumping sound against the wooden floor of my house. He seemed to relax. Then, never taking his eyes off me, he moved toward the Shaffers' house.

I watched.

But when he disappeared around the side of my house, I climbed out. I peeked around the corner of the doghouse and saw him kneeling down at the back door. He took a tool out of his pocket and started wiggling the doorknob. I could hear a jingling sound, but I really couldn't see what he was doing. I moved closer to watch.

The man worked and worked. Finally he glanced around. When he saw me standing right next to him, a little squeal came from his throat. He jumped so hard he landed on his bottom beside the back door.

"Nice doggy." His voice shook as hard as he

did. "Don't bite me." He put his hands up in front of his face. "Nice doggy."

The strange odor was very strong. It came from the man in the stocking cap. The smell sort of hurt my nose, but at the same time it made me feel big and strong inside. It was weird!

"I won't bite you," I assured him. "I'm nice. I learned my lesson with my last master. I'll never bite anything or anybody ever again."

But, like most people, I guess he just didn't understand Dog. He kept his hands up and kept shaking for a long, long time. At last, when I kept wagging my tail and smiling at him, he crawled back to his knees and jiggled the door-knob some more.

I watched.

He opened the door and went into the Shaffers' house. I could hear him rattling around inside. Every now and then I could see the glow from the little light he held in his hand. After a while he came out the door.

I watched.

He carried a big sack to the back fence and lifted it over. Then, still shaking and smiling at me, he came back to the house.

I watched as he carried another bag to the back fence, then another. When he climbed over the last time, he waved at me.

"You dumb mutt. You're the kind of watchdog that I love."

I smiled back at him and waved good-bye with my tail. I didn't really like being called a dumb mutt, but the way he laughed and smiled made me feel good. In fact, I could hear him laughing and chuckling as he dragged the heavy bags all the way across the sandy field behind my yard. Besides, he did say that I was the kind of watchdog that he loved. That made me feel great.

More than anything else in the whole world, being a good watchdog was the one thing I wanted. I guess I'd done a good job, too. I knew my new master, Mr. Shaffer, would be very proud of me, because . . .

I watched—just like a good watchdog is supposed to.

Chapter 2

"**I**'m going straight to the pound," I whined. "This is it. There's nothing else left. I'm a goner."

I paced up and down by the fence along my side yard. I didn't know what the pound was like, but I remember Scotty whining and crying when his master was about to take him there. I remember that I never saw him again. Whatever the pound was, it was bad.

"This is it," I whimpered. "He's gone in to get my collar, and when he comes back out . . ."

My tail tucked under my belly. My floppy ears drooped so low they almost dragged on the ground.

"What are you whining about?"

I jerked. The growl from the other side of the fence startled me. My droopy ears perked up.

"Who's there?"

"What are you whining about?" the voice repeated. It was Red, the Irish setter who lived in the yard next to mine.

I'd never seen Red because of the wooden fence. In fact, this was the first time he'd ever talked to me in the whole two months since he had moved next door with his family. I'd tried to talk with him before, but he only snarled at me through the cracks between the fence boards.

It was good to hear another voice. Besides, I was in so much trouble that I really needed someone to talk to, even if it was someone who only growled.

I squinted, trying to see through one of the cracks.

"I messed up," I told the fence. "I messed up bad, and I don't even know how it happened."

Red hair and one white eyeball appeared at the crack.

"I saw the cars with the red and blue lights on top last night," Red said. "The men in the blue uniforms kept going in and out of the house, and your master kept yelling. What did you do, get inside and tear the living room up or something?"

"No!" I shook my head so hard my ears flopped against my cheeks. "I'm a watchdog. I don't go inside."

"So what did you do?"

"I did what I was supposed to do." I shrugged both ears. "I watched."

Red growled, "Exactly *what* did you watch?"

I folded my tail under my bottom and sat down. "Well," I began, staring at the eyeball. "Last night I was watching, just like I'm supposed to. A little while after dark, this man dressed all in black climbed over the back fence. He kept wiggling something at the door, and finally he went inside."

"What did you do?"

"I watched," I answered, wiggling my whiskers. "I watched him bring a big sack out of the house and lift it over the fence."

"Then what?"

"I watched him bring out two more sacks."

Red snorted. "And you watched, right?"

I smiled. "Right."

"That's all you did?"

I twitched my whiskers. "That's what I'm supposed to do. I watched because I'm a *watchdog.*"

"You didn't growl or bark at him?"

"Oh, no. Dogs get in trouble for barking and growling."

"You didn't bite him?"

"Heaven forbid! I never bite. *Never!*"

There was a strange *whoompf* from the other side of the fence. I pressed my eye closer to the crack. Red had fallen on his side. He rolled back and forth. He wagged his tail and laughed and laughed and laughed.

"It's not funny," I whined. "I'm in trouble. My master's probably going to take me to . . . to . . . the pound."

Red just kept rolling and laughing. Finally he got to his feet and told me to follow him to the back corner of the yard. Once we got there he started digging.

"Dogs shouldn't dig," I warned him. "You'll get in trouble."

Red dug faster.

"No, I won't," he said. "The bushes are thick here. My master won't see the hole or the dirt. Even if he does, he won't get mad. Besides, you need help. You're the most confused, messed-up pup I've ever met."

My ears drooped, and my tail folded under my tummy. "Please don't dig. I had a friend named Scotty. He was a digger. His master took him to the pound. And when you go to the pound . . . well, no one ever comes back from the . . . the *pound!*"

12

Chapter 3

*T*he sand was soft. Within a few moments Red's nose appeared under the fence. More dirt flew and splattered the shrubs, and he had made a hole deep enough for him to squeeze through.

When he stood up on my side of the fence, he kind of grunted and stretched. "Man, I'm getting too old for all that hard work."

Red didn't look quite the way I had pictured him from my view through the crack in the fence. He wasn't nearly as tall as me, but he was still sleek and trim. He had long red hair, except for the tufts around his forehead and whiskers. There his coat was beginning to turn white with age.

He moaned again and wiggled so the sand would fall off his belly. After that, he sniffed me all over. Then he explored my yard and came back to sniff me again.

He folded his tail to the side and sat down on one hip. "Well," he announced after his inspection. "You're no coward. You're big, but you're just as gentle as you said you were." He cocked a red ear. "You're not stupid, either—but you sure are mixed up."

I tilted my head to the side. "You can tell all that from sniffing?"

"Listen, pup. When you get to be my age you learn to tell a lot about dogs—and people—from a good sniff."

A shudder made the hair on my back bristle as I looked at the hole Red had left under my fence. "We should hide," I whimpered. "I'm in trouble already. When my master sees the hole you made"—I swallowed and shook all over—"I'll probably get sent to the pound. I don't want you to get sent there, too."

"Every time you mention the pound, your smell of fear hurts my nose," Red snorted. "My master's not gonna send me to the pound."

"Are you sure?"

"Of course I'm sure." Red yawned. "Long time ago I was running in the pasture with him and his boy. We found this pond, and I jumped in. I love the water. Only thing Irish setters love more than running is swimming. Anyway, his boy— dumb kid—decides to jump in with me. Idiot didn't know how to swim.

"Well, he started flopping around and screaming, so I paddled over to see what his problem was. Little rascal latched on to my tail. Only thing for me to do was paddle for the bank. Either that or let the kid drown both of us. My master got there just as I was dragging his boy up on the bank. I guess he figured the kid fell in and I jumped in to save him—neither one of 'em was ever too bright. Anyway, since that day I've never had to worry about anything. I can dig in the dirt, I can wet on the carpet, I can even chew up the garden hose—he never gets mad at me. Thinks I'm the greatest dog that ever lived. So quit worrying about the hole. It's not a problem. You're the one with the problem."

I nodded and sat down on my haunches to face him.

"You're right," I sighed. "I really do have a problem. This is my third master. The other two got mad at me and gave me away. My friend Scotty told me that he was on his third master— but when his master got mad at him, he didn't give him away. He took him to the *pound*. Now

15

my master's mad at me and . . . and . . ." I sniffed. "And I don't even know what I did wrong."

Red flipped his tail to the side and rocked to his other hip.

"The guy you told me about, the one all dressed in black—that was a burglar. He must have taken things from your master's house. That's why all the cars with the red and blue lights showed up after your master got home. Why didn't you stop the guy?"

"How?"

Red cocked his ears and tilted his head. "Bite him, you dunce! Take a chunk out of his leg. Growl at him. Chase him off."

I fell to the ground and covered my head with my paws. "Oh, that's a terrible idea," I whimpered. "I can't bite. That's why my last master gave me away. I promised then that I'd never bite another living thing as long as I lived."

Remembering made me hurt inside. My tail tucked under. My head hung low, and my ears drooped so tight against the sides of my face that I couldn't even hear the desert wind.

Gently Red reached down with his nose and lifted one of my ears. "Calm down, pup," he soothed. "It can't be all that bad. Tell me about it. Start at the very beginning."

Chapter 4

*W*hen Red told me to start at the beginning, he probably didn't mean the *very* beginning. But that was when my problems had really started, so I told him about how I was the biggest puppy my mama had ever had. She told me that of her two litters, I was by far the greatest Great Dane ever. I guess that's why my brothers and sisters complained so much and why they called me a bully. When they shoved for the best sleeping spot, I shoved back. When they tried to muscle in for Mama's best milk, I wouldn't budge. Since I was so big, I always got what I wanted.

"When we played and wrestled and bit each other," I told Red, "even if I was trying to be gentle, they yapped and squealed because I bit too hard." With my paw, I brushed my whiskers. The memories made me so sad that even my whiskers drooped. "I didn't try to be mean. I was just big—it wasn't really my fault. But . . . well, it always hurt when they called me a bully, so I tried my very best not to hurt them when we played. I guess I should have figured out then that I was just too big to bite, even if it was only play-biting.

"Mama was the only one who really liked me. She used to look real proud when she said how big I was. Whenever I chased the sparrows away from her food bowl, she told me that someday I'd be a great watchdog."

I looked up at Red.

"That's what I've always wanted to be. As long as I can remember, I wanted to make my mama proud. I wanted to be a great watchdog. That's what I did last night. I watched."

Red lay down and rested his chin on his paws so he could look me straight in the eye. "To be a good watchdog, you got to do more than just *watch*. Now, I understand that your brothers and sisters calling you a bully hurt your feelings, but that doesn't explain the panic you went into when I asked why you didn't bite the burglar. There's got to be more to it than what you're telling me. The least you could have done is bark at him."

I covered my eyes with my paws. Red pushed them aside. "Tell me. Maybe talking about it will help."

The very thought was enough to make me whimper. I forced back the sound and tickled my whiskers with my long tongue.

"My first master was a little boy," I began. "Well, he wasn't a little boy, he was a *big* little boy. We lived in California, and he used to tie a red bandanna around my neck and take me to the beach. I'd run and romp, and when girls would pet me and say how big and nice I was, he'd come up and flirt with them. We had a good thing going.

"Only, like I said, he was a big little boy. I was still a puppy when he went away to this place called college. I missed him. I'd get so lonely I couldn't stand it. At night I'd cry and howl. The daddy didn't like that. He yelled at me. He even threw water on me. The neighbors had a cat. Sometimes the cat would come over and climb on our roof. Sometimes cars would park in the alley behind our house. Every time the cat climbed on our roof or the cars parked in the alley, I barked to warn the daddy what was going on. He never understood, though. Each time I

19

barked or howled, he'd yell at me or throw water on me. Even the neighbors yelled at me and threw stuff. They yelled at the daddy, too."

"People are kind of dumb animals," Red sighed. "They really can't communicate too well. So what happened next?"

"So," I continued, "one day this lady came to the house. I barked to tell the daddy that someone was there. She looked mean and acted funny. I growled at her, and she kicked me. Then she started pounding on the door. When the daddy didn't come, she started yanking on the doorknob and trying to get in. I was afraid she was going to hurt the daddy. So . . . so . . ."

"So?"

I sniffed. "So I bit her. I nipped her right on her big flabby bottom. I figured it would make her go away. Only she didn't go away. She started screaming and crying and yelling. The daddy came running out the door. He kept yelling at me and hitting me with a rolled-up magazine. He told me that if I ever bit his mother again, he'd take me straight to the pound." I looked at Red and swallowed the big knot that lumped up in my throat. "I didn't know she was his mama. I was just trying to protect him."

Red gave a little sigh. "It was an honest mistake. It really wasn't your fault."

"That's what I tried to tell him, only—"

"Yeah," Red knew what I was going to say. "Only he didn't understand Dog."

I nodded. "About a week after that, the daddy's brother came to visit from Oklahoma. He had a little little boy who came out and played with me in the backyard. He was real tiny, so I was careful not to knock him down and stuff. I really liked him, too. Anyway, the daddy told his brother that I needed a boy to play with, and since they lived on a farm in the country, my barking wouldn't bother the neighbors. He never mentioned that I had bitten his mother. The brother took me to live with them in Oklahoma."

Red rolled to his side and rested his cheek on the ground. "You bit somebody else when you got to Oklahoma, right?"

My ears twitched. "Well, no. Not really."

"You barked at stuff or you . . ."

Suddenly Red stopped and stared at the fence on the far side of my yard.

"Who's that?"

"That's Poky," I told him. "He and his master just moved into that new house two days ago."

"What is he?"

I shrugged. "Don't know. He won't talk to me. When I tried to make friends, he growled and told

21

me how big he was and how mean and terrible, and he said if he ever got ahold of me, he'd chew my head off."

"You ever see him?"

"No. The fence boards on that side are too close together. I can't see through them at all. But I know he's big and really mean. He told me so."

Red snorted. He made that grunting sound when he stood up. I followed him across the yard.

"Hi. My name's Red. I'm an Irish setter. This is my friend—"

"Get away from my yard!" The smell and the high, sharp growl from the other side of the fence warned us. "Back off or I'll rip both of you to shreds. I'm big and tough and mean."

Red's white eyebrows scrunched low on his red forehead. "You sound and smell like a beagle."

There was another growl from the far side of the fence. "Yeah, that's right. But I'm huge. I'm the biggest, meanest beagle you ever saw, and if you mess with me I'll—"

"Nobody's gonna mess with you," Red snorted. "I'm too old to fight, and this pup here is nothin' but a big pussycat."

"I'm not a pussycat," I pouted. "I'm a Great Dane."

"Some Great Dane," Red huffed. "You may

think you're a Great Dane. You may think you're a watchdog, but you act like a pussycat."

Through the fence, he explained to Poky what had happened with the burglar last night. Poky just growled at him. Red told him that he had dug a hole under my fence so we could be friends and he could help me. Poky only snarled.

Red confided in him that even though he was old, he still got lonely and figured it would be nice to have a friend. "Since I'm out making friends, I figure I might as well make friends with you, too."

"I don't want to make friends," Poky barked. "I'm too big and mean to have friends."

Red looked at me and winked. "We'll just see."

With that, he trotted to the corner where my back fence joined the side where Poky lived. My eyes flashed in terror as he started to dig. I was going to the pound for sure. Not only had I messed up and let the burglar in, but now there was going to be a huge hole in my backyard and I'd get blamed for it.

Chapter 5

"*P*lease!" I whimpered. "Don't dig a hole in my yard. Mr. Shaffer will take me to the pound and . . ."

Red ignored me and kept digging.

I had to stop him. I remembered what had happened to Scotty. I couldn't let Red dig. In the twitch of a whisker, I leaped between him and the fence. I plopped down, right where he was digging.

He looked at me and snarled. Then, with a grunt, he pulled his paws out from under my bottom.

"Move, you big ox!" he growled.

Red tried to dig under my tail. I pushed my

bottom harder against the ground. "Please stop. If Mr. Shaffer finds a hole in his yard—"

"Get away from my yard," the high voice snarled from the far side of the tall fence.

Red moved around in front of me and started digging from a different angle. I put my front paws down and stopped him.

"I'm warning you!" Poky yapped. "I'm big and tough and mean and . . ."

Red moved again. He tried to wiggle himself between me and the fence so he could dig. I pushed against him and kept him from getting through. Instantly he scooted behind me and tried to dig there. He shoved, trying to make an opening between me and the fence. I pushed harder against the fence to block him.

There was a loud *crunch-crack!*

Something snapped. Something gave way. I felt myself falling. Paws and legs sprawling, I tumbled backwards. I landed on my head with a thud.

Suddenly I was no longer in my yard. I blinked and looked around. The fence was on the wrong side. I was on the wrong side! I was upside down!

From the corner of my eye I saw a white, black, and brown streak. It shot across the yard and disappeared into a small doghouse under a pecan tree.

Paws churning, I rolled from my back and struggled to my feet. Frantic, I looked all around.

"Where am I? What happened? Where's my yard and my food bowl?"

"Good job, pup!" Red's head appeared through an opening in the fence. Then his shoulders, chest, and rear. Finally his tail slipped through and he wagged it. "Wish I was big enough to snap boards like that. It would sure save a lot of time and effort digging under."

"What happened?" I repeated.

Red turned back to the fence. With his nose, he shoved on one of the boards. It swung from a loose nail at the top. As it moved, I could see the fresh wood at the bottom where it was cracked. The two boards next to it were broken as well, although I could barely see the crack. They were also held by one loose nail at the top of the fence.

"You snapped those three boards, pup. Just busted right through 'em. Those loose boards make a neat gate. The way they swing from those top nails—as soon as we go through, they just slip back in place. Our masters won't even know about it."

"But how do I get home?" One ear arched.

"Just stick your nose through the crack," Red explained. "Once you squeeze through, the fence boards just swing back in place. I couldn't have done it better myself."

I stuck my nose in the crack. Sure enough the board moved over. I was so big that two boards moved when I thrust my whole head through. My yard was still there. So was my food bowl.

Just then someone nipped my tail. It was a gentle nip, more of a tug. I backed out of the opening and looked around.

Red tugged my tail again.

"Come on. Let's go check out the beagle."

I hesitated. The beagle, Poky, was big and mean and scary. I really didn't know whether we should try to find him or not.

Red trotted across the yard toward the little doghouse under the pecan tree. I waited a moment, then cautiously followed him.

"Why did you lie to me?" I asked.

The little dog cowered against the back wall of the tiny doghouse. He covered one eye with a big floppy ear. Poky was tiny. Well, I guess he was the normal size for a beagle, but compared to me he was tiny. He was mostly white with big black and brown spots on his fur. It would have taken five of him to make one of me, and he wasn't mean at all.

"Why did you lie?" I repeated. "You told me you were big and fierce and mean."

The floppy ear wiggled just a bit. I could see part of a soft brown eye.

"I could tell you were huge," Poky said sheepishly. "I was afraid if you knew how small I was, you'd eat me. So . . . well, I figured if you thought I was big and mean and tough, you'd stay on your own side of the fence. I really am tough, though. I'm a lot stronger and meaner than I look." Again, he hid his eye under his ear. "Please don't eat me."

Red plopped down on his bottom. He had to lean over to see inside the low doghouse. "Nobody's gonna eat you. We just want to be friends. Come on out."

Red and I talked to Poky for a long, long, long time before we finally got him out of his house. When he did come out, he tried to look mean. His curved tail stood straight up in the air. The hair rose along his back in a sharp ridge, and his little short legs were as stiff as the boards in the fence.

We all took turns sniffing and inspecting each other. Poky kept growling and telling us how ferocious he was. But he finally relaxed.

"I guess you guys are okay," he admitted. "You're just so darned big, though."

29

"I'm a Great Dane," I told him. "Great Danes are supposed to be big. We can't help it."

"I'm not all that big," Red confessed. "I'm really kind of skinny—mostly long red hair. Besides, like I told you through the fence, I'm too old to fight. And the pup here is nothing but a big ol' pussycat."

"I'm not a pussycat," I said. "I'm a dog. And I'm not a pup, either. I'm three and a half years old, so I'm an adult dog."

Red wiggled his nose from side to side. "Well, compared to me, you're a pup. I'm twelve. Besides, you act like a pup—won't even bite a burglar."

"A burglar!" Poky snarled. "Is that what all the commotion was last night? Man, if I ever get ahold of a burglar, I'll chew his leg off."

While we explored Poky's yard and peed on his shrubs, Red told him all about the burglar and why I didn't bite him because I made a mistake once and bit some old lady on the bottom. When the three of us squeezed through the boards to show Poky my yard and pee on my bushes, Red told him about how my brothers and sisters called me a bully and about how I was afraid to dig in the dirt because of this guy named Scotty who got sent to the pound.

We were just getting ready to crawl through

the hole so we could explore Red's yard when Poky stopped. His floppy ears perked up and his tail stopped wagging.

"That's my master's car. It's almost evening, and he's home from work." His tail made a circle. "My master will be out to feed me any minute now."

Red glanced at the orange sliver of sun that rested on the back fence. "We'd better get home before our masters find out we've been gone," he said. "First thing after they leave for work in the morning, we'll get together and see if we can straighten this pussycat—excuse me, Great Dane—we'll see if we can straighten him out."

Poky slipped through the opening on his side of the yard. As soon as his tail disappeared, the boards fell back into place as if they weren't even broken. Red made a grunting sound as he squeezed through the hole on his side of the yard.

"I figure you're safe," he called from the other side. "If your master was going to take you to the pound, he would have already done it, so quit worrying. See you in the morning, pup."

"My name's not pup," I told the fence. "It's Sweetie."

From the other side of the boards, I could hear Red chuckling.

31

Chapter 6

*T*hat night a coyote howled in the desert. He was much closer than the last time I'd heard him. The sound of his voice made me uneasy. His howl made the hair on my back stand on end. He was so close that I could almost understand what he was howling about—almost but not quite. The sound didn't make me feel lonely, though. Now, I had two new friends. Friends make you feel better.

I guess Red was right about my master. Mr. Shaffer didn't take me to the pound. In fact, the next morning he even petted me and scratched behind my ears when he put my dog food in my bowl. "Some watchdog you are," he said.

His words should have made my tail wag, but the way he said the word "watchdog" made my shoulders sag and my tail tuck under. I knew for sure that my master was not really proud of me. People are bad about that, I thought. They're bad about saying one thing when they really mean something else.

When Poky's master left for work, the beagle shoved the broken boards aside with his nose and came over to say good morning. We waited at the hole under Red's fence until we heard a door slam and a car pull out of the driveway. Then we went to visit Red.

Poky walked right through the hole under the fence. He hardly had to squat down. I couldn't get through. I was afraid to dig, so I waited by the fence until Red and Poky dug enough dirt out of the hole for me to squeeze my way under. We explored Red's yard and romped and even chased one another around and around the yard. Even though he was old, Red was still pretty fast. He got tired quickly, though, so we went to sit by his doghouse.

"Got plenty of food left," he panted. "You guys hungry? Help yourselves."

"I'm always hungry." Poky wagged his tail. "Thanks." Then he looked up at me. "How about you? You're as big as a horse. Probably takes a ton of dog food to fill you up. You go first."

I flipped my tail to the side and sat down. "I may look as big as a horse to you, but that doesn't mean I have to eat like one. I'm full. You eat. I'm not hungry."

Poky finished Red's leftovers. Then all three of us stretched out to soak up some of the warm sunshine.

We spent that day and the days that followed lying in the sun and playing chase. Red wouldn't run for very long because he got tired. Poky had lots more energy. He was quick, too. Just about the time I got to him, he'd dart to the side. My long legs were faster than his short stubby ones, but I couldn't turn as quickly. I nearly had to stop to make such sharp turns. Sometimes he'd turn so quickly that I'd stumble and land on my chin just trying to keep up with him.

I *did* have to be careful not to step on Poky. My paws were so big, and he was so small—one good smack might have smushed him.

I was glad that Red had forgotten to make me tell him about my little little boy. The memories of my boy and of Oklahoma always made me sad. I was having so much fun with my new friends. I wanted the good feelings to last, and I wanted to forget the sad times.

And we did have some wonderful times. We spent the fall romping and playing. We shared our food. We chased each other and lay in the yard to soak up the warm Arizona sun.

Winter tried to come a couple of times, but fall chased it away as quickly and easily as I used to chase the sparrows away from Mama's food bowl. I knew it would be that way, too.

The first year I lived with the Shaffers was in a place called Chickasha, Oklahoma. The winter there was cold and nasty. It rained, and a few times it snowed or the ground was slippery with ice. When the wind blew from the north, it howled! It shook the brown leaves from the trees and left them naked and shivering. It was a damp, cold wind that seemed to cut right through my fur and down to my very bones.

Then, two years ago, my master got a new job—it was called retirement. We moved here, to Scottsdale. Mr. and Mrs. Shaffer worked hard at retirement. She painted pictures, and he made things out of silver and pretty little blue stones. Each morning they got in their car and went to the shop. I didn't know what the shop was, but they always took their pictures and trinkets with them, and they always came home about the same time Poky's master did.

The two years we'd spent at Mr. Shaffer's new

job in Arizona had been great. The winters here seemed more like spring in Oklahoma. The wind didn't blow, and there was never ice on the ground to slip and fall on. I thought it would always be that way.

Only, this winter was different.

One night the wind howled. It was so cold that even the needles on the cactuses shivered. I kept hearing this strange sound, so I crawled out of my warm doghouse to investigate. The sound came from the direction of Red's yard. I leaned my ear against the wood fence and listened. It was a whining, whimpering sort of sound. It was Red's voice. It sounded as if he was hurt.

Quick as a flash, I darted under the fence and trotted to his doghouse. Red was huddled in the corner. He was asleep, but his legs shook and the whimpering sound kept coming from his half-open mouth.

"Red?"

He just trembled.

"Red," I said louder, "are you all right?"

One eye opened. He jerked, surprised to see my big head poked into his doghouse.

"What's wrong, Red? Are you hurt?"

"It's my arthritis," he moaned. "I didn't mean to wake you."

37

I cocked an ear and tilted my head to the side. "What's arthritis?"

He whined and straightened his front leg. "It's my joints. People get it, too. That's how I learned the word. My master is always moaning and complaining about his arthritis. It happens to us sometimes when we get old. Our joints get stiff, and they hurt. I guess the cold brought it on."

I nudged him with my nose. "I can help keep you warm," I said. I started to crawl through the doorway. Red's house wasn't nearly as big as mine. There wasn't room.

"Can you get up?"

Red moved his legs and groaned. I nudged him again. "Come on over to my house. There's plenty of room. We can snuggle up, and I'll help keep you warm. You won't hurt so much if you're warm."

It took the Irish setter a long time to get up. On stiff straight legs, he followed me to the hole under our fence. He let out a little yelp and moaned when he bent down to squeeze through. Once we were both in my house, I gave Red the spot I had already warmed up. Then I lay down and kind of made a curve around him so I could keep him warm. For a time, he moaned and whined. I snuggled closer, and after a while Red relaxed and fell asleep.

Once I was sure he was warm and comfortable, I dozed, too. Tomorrow night, if it was still cold, I would invite Poky to come and sleep with us. It felt good to have a friend to snuggle up with. I don't think I ever slept so well. It was the best sleep I could ever remember.

Until . . .

Chapter 7

The loud, awful sound of snarling and yapping and barking shook me from my sound sleep. I jumped when I heard the terrible noise. My head clunked the top of my doghouse.

I shook the pain away and frowned, wondering what all the noise was.

"What's going on?" Red moaned.

"Don't know. I'll go see."

I squeezed through the doorway of my doghouse and stretched.

"That's my bone!" Poky's angry voice came from the other side of the fence. "You leave it alone."

There was more snarling.

"That's my food bowl! You get away from it!"

Red poked his head out through my doorway. "What's going on over in Poky's yard?"

"Don't know." I shrugged my ears. "But Poky sounds very upset about something." I took a couple of steps toward the fence. "Poky? Poky, what's wrong?"

"Coyotes!"

"Coyotes?"

"Coyotes!" Poky screamed again. "You and Red get over here quick! There's a whole pack of them. It will take all three of us to fight them off."

Red tumbled out of my doghouse. He was so stiff and sore he could barely get to his feet.

"Come on," he yapped. "We have to help."

I followed him toward the broken boards.

Suddenly there was a loud growl from Poky's yard.

"Leave that alone! Get away from my food or I'm going to bite you."

"We're not scared of you," a strange voice snarled back. "If you bite us, we'll eat you up instead of just taking your food."

"I got friends," Poky barked. "You get out right now, or they'll come over here and eat *you* up."

The coyotes only laughed.

It took Red forever to limp across the yard.

41

He shoved the boards aside with his nose and stumbled through.

"Look!" a coyote yapped. "Another dog. He's big. Run!"

"Nah," another coyote scoffed. "Look at him. He's so old and crippled he ain't gonna bother us. Let's finish eating."

I reached for the board with my nose. I hesitated.

What if the coyotes didn't leave Poky alone? What if they tried to bite us? My legs shook. I couldn't bite them back if they bit me. I don't bite. Maybe I better not go through the hole.

But when I heard more snarling and growling followed by a sudden painful shriek from Poky, I shoved the boards aside and squeezed through the hole.

The coyotes scattered.

Three of them leaped over the back fence. But when the two others saw that I wasn't chasing them, they stopped. They crouched in the corners of the yard. They hid in the shadows.

I could hardly see them. But I did see their yellow eyes, which caught the light from the big moon. I saw how their white teeth shone, too. Drool glistened as it dripped from their snarling mouths. That was all I could see of them.

As I watched, I felt the hair rise in a ridge along

my back. Something from deep inside made my rage boil. Without knowing why, I trembled. That smell—the same one I had smelled from the man in the stocking cap—swept into my nostrils. It wiggled my nose, but at the same time the smell made me feel big and strong. My lip started to curl, and I bared my fangs.

Suddenly I caught myself. I was ashamed of the way I was acting. I took a deep breath and forced the hair to lie down on my back. I replaced the snarl on my lips with a smile.

Poky raced between Red and me. His legs were stiff. The hair stuck out in a sharp line down his back.

"Go get 'em, Sweetie! Go tear 'em up!"

I made the smile stay on my lips. I forced my tail to wag. "Is there a problem, here?" I asked calmly. "Is there something I can do to help?"

Poky snarled.

"Yeah, there's a problem. Those stinking coyotes are stealing my food. One of the guys that jumped over the fence took my best bone with him. Go get 'em, Sweetie. Eat 'em up!"

"Now, Poky," I soothed. "You know I don't bite. Let's see if we can talk this out. Let's try to be friends."

Poky's mouth flopped open. His head tilted to

one side, and an ear drooped so low it almost touched the ground.

"Friends!" he gasped. "With *coyotes?*"

"Of course," I nodded. "Friends are great. You can never have too many friends."

"But coyotes . . . !"

I ignored him and turned toward the yellow eyes and white fangs in the corner. "Hello. My name is Sweetie. I'd like to be your friend."

The coyote only growled. His yellow eyes squinted.

I shrugged. "I'm sure you know stealing is wrong. You didn't really mean to take Poky's food without his permission, did you?"

A very big coyote who was hiding in the far corner of Poky's yard took a step forward.

"It's been a very cold winter," he growled. "The rabbits are all gone. We can't find any lizards, and the people used a big machine to cover up all the garbage at the dump. We're hungry."

"Oh," I gasped, "that's terrible. I've never been hungry, but I'm sure it must be awful." I reached out a paw and laid it lightly on Poky's shoulder. "My friend here is a good dog. I'm sure if you had only told him that, he would have been glad to share his food with you."

"What?" Poky's eyes popped wide. "I can't believe you said that." He dropped his shoulder and

shook my paw off. "Share with thieving coyotes? You must be nuts!"

With that, he spun around. His nose in the air on one end and his tail in the air on the other, he trotted on stiff legs back to his doghouse. There he stood beside his food bowl and took a deep breath, trying to make himself look big.

"It's my food," he growled. "You know I always get hungry for a midnight snack. If they steal my food, I won't have any. I ain't sharin'. I'll fight for it before I let them steal any more."

My ears sagged. I heaved a deep sigh and sat down on my haunches. Red limped toward Poky. "Come on, Sweetie. Let's help the little guy."

I didn't follow him.

The big coyote took a step. I stood up. The coyote drew back his paw and trembled.

"Stealing is wrong!" I told the big coyote.

"No, it's not. It's the way we coyotes live. We take whatever we find. We get it any way we can. If we're smart enough and sneaky enough to take it, then it's ours. That ain't stealing."

I turned and shoved one of the boards aside in the fence.

"Then you can have some of my food. I don't have much left, but I will be glad to share it with you. That way we can be friends."

The coyotes only glared at me.

45

WATCHDOG AND THE COYOTES

After a long, long time, I finally gave up. If no one was willing to talk, the only thing for me to do was go home and get some sleep. I squeezed through the broken boards and curled up in my doghouse.

Things were quiet for a long time. Suddenly there was a little growl. Then: *"Yowieee!"*

I watched.

Poky shot through the broken boards with his tail tucked between his legs. Red limped after him. Poky raced across the yard and hid behind my doghouse. Red went through the hole and hid in his own house.

I crawled out of my house and went to see what was the matter.

"He bit me," Poky panted. "He bit me, and they stole the rest of my food and my chewy bone. Why didn't you help me?"

I leaned my cheek against the doghouse. "I tried. I offered to share my food with them."

Poky licked the little hole on his hind leg where the coyote had nipped him. "You can't share with coyotes," he snorted. "They don't know how to share. You give them a little bit and they take everything. You should have helped me."

His big brown eyes looked very sad. He stared

47

straight up at me and sniffed. "You should have helped me."

With that, he limped off and slipped through the broken boards. His head hung so low that his long, droopy ears dragged on the ground.

All alone, I crawled into my doghouse. I felt so sad and helpless that my ears dragged on the ground, too.

Chapter 8

For the next three nights things were quiet and peaceful. Poky wouldn't talk to me. Red stayed pretty much to himself. He wouldn't come through the hole under the fence, and when I went to see him, he said the same thing Poky had: "You should have helped. I tried, but I'm too old and weak. They were going to bite me, too. You should have helped us."

Then he curled up in his house and wouldn't talk to me, either.

On the fourth night, the coyotes howled.

They were far off in the desert, but this time I could understand them. They howled about how hard life was and how they'd always been poor and hungry. They howled for the rabbits or any other animals to come out of their burrows. Because, as the coyotes put it, "You owe it to us! We won't hurt you. We'll just eat you. We *deserve* to be fed."

They howled about how there was no justice in the world and how unfair it was for dogs and cats and people and horses and sheep to have homes and barns to sleep in, while coyotes had to sleep in a hole in the ground.

And they howled and howled and howled.

The next night they came back. This time there were six of them.

Poky didn't try to fight them. Instead, he shot through the hole in the fence and hid behind my doghouse.

I went to Poky's yard to investigate. The big coyote with sharp white fangs met me.

I tried to talk with him. I offered to share my food with him. He only called me a big coward and told me to get lost.

It was a cold night. When the coyotes finished eating what was left of Poky's food, three of them curled up and went to sleep in his doghouse. I went back to my house and invited Poky to come inside and sleep with me. Poky didn't even answer. He stayed behind my house, pouting.

The coyotes came again the next night. This

time, they came right after dark. They got there before Poky had a chance to eat any of the food his master had set out for him. They spent the whole evening sleeping in his doghouse while Poky shivered in the cold.

They came back the next night, too. This time, instead of six, there were eight.

Three of them ate Poky's food and slept in his doghouse. The other five jumped over the back fence of Red's yard.

When Red called for help, Poky just thumped his tail on the ground. "He wouldn't help me," Poky huffed. "Said he was too old and sore. Darned if I'll help him."

"He *is* old, Poky. It's not his fault."

Poky just ignored me, so I went to see if there was anything I could do. I crouched down at the hole and stuck my head under the fence. Two coyotes stood there. One of them snapped at my nose. I jerked my head back. The coyote's teeth missed my snout by only inches. When I offered to share my food with them, they just laughed and called me a coward and told me to get lost.

Red tried to fight, but he was old and weak. It wasn't long before he came tearing under the fence.

"Why didn't you help me fight them?" he

asked, puffing and panting and all out of breath. "You should have helped."

Red went to the back of my doghouse. I followed, my ears dragging on the ground. Poky wouldn't have anything to do with Red or me. He slept in the middle of the yard.

After two days, my friends got hungry. We shared my food, and for three more nights the coyotes slept in Poky's and Red's houses and ate their food. They always came just after sundown and left before our people woke up in the morning. That way our masters never saw them.

One bowl of dog food wasn't much for three dogs. I ate very little. I didn't want my friends to be hungry. My insides felt empty. At night my tummy would growl. It growled so loud that it echoed in my doghouse and woke me. I didn't mind, though. I couldn't let my friends go hungry, and . . . I couldn't chase the coyotes away. I just couldn't bite.

The next night, the coyotes came back. This time there were ten.

Two coyotes went to Poky's yard. They ate his food and went to sleep in his house. Two went to Red's yard. They ate his food and slept in his house. The others crept through the holes on either side of my yard.

We had just started eating when they got there.

"He *is* big," one of the coyotes whispered as they crept closer to me.

"Yeah," answered the largest coyote, who I figured was the leader. "But he's nothing but a big coward. Come on."

Poky and Red tried to gobble down as much food as they could. They were very, very hungry. Bravely I turned to face the coyotes alone. I walked toward them.

"I am not a coward," I protested. "I don't bite because I want to be your friend."

The biggest coyote smiled. It looked more like a sneer. "See?" he told his friend. "What did I tell you?"

"Yeah," the smaller coyote said. "But he sure is big. I wonder how big he is?"

The leader pranced right up beside me. He told his friend to jump on his back. Standing, one on top of the other, the two coyotes came up to my shoulders.

I stood and watched them. "Why have you come? What do you want here?"

The coyote on top licked his lips. "Two bowls of dog food isn't enough for ten coyotes. We're still hungry. We want more."

While they were talking, the other four coyotes sneaked around behind me and chased Red and

53

Poky away from my bowl. The coyotes started to eat.

"I'm sorry you're hungry," I said. "But if you eat Red's food and Poky's food *and* my food, then what will we have to eat?"

"That's your problem." The coyote on bottom laughed.

"But we'll starve," I said.

"So?"

"So that's not right."

The coyote on top jumped down. "It's right for us. We take what we want. You dogs got a lot. You got plenty of food and nice houses to sleep in. We got nothin'. We want what *you* got. We deserve it."

"Deserve it? Why?"

The big coyote moved up beside me. With his shoulder, he shoved me out of the way.

"We've been poor for a long, long time—that's why! We eat rabbits and mice and lizards and berries. We even have to eat cactus sometimes, and garbage from the trash pile. We deserve better, and we're going to take it."

With that, he shoved me again. I staggered sideways and watched the two coyotes join their friends at my bowl.

For the next two nights we slept in my yard. The second night was terribly cold, and for the

first time in a long, long while we huddled together for warmth.

The coyotes ate our food. They gobbled it down and laughed. They slobbered and burped. Then they crawled into our warm, cozy doghouses and laughed and talked some more. All the while Poky, Red, and I lay shivering on the cold, cold ground. I never imagined things could get worse.

Chapter 9

The growling from our three empty tummies woke us early the next morning. Red struggled to his feet and tried to stretch. Sleeping on the cold ground made him stiffer than ever.

"We've got to do something," he whimpered. "We're gonna starve to death if we don't."

Poky got up and shook his curved tail. "What can we do? I'm too little. Sweetie won't even growl at a fly, much less bite one. You're too old and scared."

"Red's not scared," I protested. "He's a brave dog."

"He's scared," Poky repeated. "I smelled it."

Red slouched. He looked down at the ground,

and when he leaned forward, his long red ears covered his eyes.

"Poky's right, Sweetie. I am scared. When I was young, I didn't know enough to be scared. When I was older, I was strong and fast, and I'd chase dogs away from my yard. Even bigger dogs didn't scare me. It was *my* yard, and I wasn't afraid of anything. Now . . ." His tail slipped under his hip and curled around his tummy. "Now I'm afraid. I'm old and weak and sore. I know if I try to take on those coyotes, they'll hurt me. I hurt enough already, just from being old. I don't want to hurt any more. They might even kill me."

As he talked, that strange but familiar smell came to my nose. It hurt, but at the same time it made me feel big and strong inside. I tilted my head and cocked one ear.

"Is that what fear smells like?" I asked.

Red shrugged. "When you're afraid, you can't smell fear."

Poky sniffed at Red. "That's the smell of fear!"

I plopped on my bottom. I sat down so quickly I forgot to move my tail out of the way. It crooked under me, and I had to shift my weight to get it out.

"I smelled it before. I tasted it. Only I didn't know what it was." I glanced at Poky. "Why didn't I smell it on you the first night the coyotes came?"

Poky's tummy growled. "I was mad. When they stole my food, then got my chewy bone, I was so mad I couldn't even see straight. That was my favorite chewy bone. I was so mad I forgot to be scared."

I looked down at my front paws, remembering.

"I smelled something very close to it from the big coyote, the leader, only it went away. I remember because it was like the smell on the burglar that night he came to my master's house." As I stared down at my paws, pictures and smells and tastes flooded the space between my ears. "I remember tasting the smell on my friend Scotty when he left for the pound—only somehow it was a little different from the smell of fear on the coyote and the burglar. And I remember my second master. The little little boy and his . . . his father and . . ."

I stopped as the sadness swept through me and made me jerk.

Red turned to me. The white hair above his eyes wiggled. "You said you'd tell me about your second master." Red yawned. "Your little boy in Oklahoma?"

I had tried not to think about that. Having all the misery of putting up with the coyotes made me feel bad enough. Thinking about my last home would make it even worse. Talking would just bring the bad feelings back again. I didn't want to tell them, but Red and Poky kept insisting.

"I was only there for three or four months," I began. "My little boy was named Ben. He was real little—only about five or so in people years. With my big little boy in California, I could romp and play. We had a blast flirting with the big little girls on the beach. When we got home, my big little boy would wrestle with me. He'd roll on the ground and tumble over me, then he'd jump up and run. I'd chase him, and we'd romp and tumble some more.

"Things were different with my little little boy. I couldn't romp and play with him 'cause he was too easy to knock over. I'd follow him around, and he'd hug my neck and pet me. I'd lick him—real careful 'cause my tongue would send him flopping backwards if I kissed him too hard. He used to try to ride on my back. It didn't hurt much, since he was so little, but if I stood up, he'd fall off and start crying. I was always real gentle with him. I really loved him."

I sighed and scratched a flea that nibbled at my empty tummy. "Ben's mama had a dog—a poodle. Her name was Fu Fu. That poodle didn't like

Ben, she hated me, and she didn't like the mama too much." I licked my whiskers and flopped my ears. "Come to think of it, I don't suppose Fu Fu even liked Fu Fu.

"Mostly she stayed in the house. But one day she had an accident on the carpet. The mama shoved her out the door into the yard where Ben and I were playing. I was polite and said hi to her, but she just stuck her little nose up in the air. Ben wanted to play with her. But she just walked off with her nose held high and snooty. Ben followed her.

"He chased her all around the yard. She growled and told him to quit. I tried to explain that all he wanted to do was play, but she didn't care. 'I hate kids!' she growled. 'Get the little stinker away from me or I'll bite him.' I didn't believe her. I guess I should have."

As I remembered that terrible day, a tear rolled from my eye. I wiped it away with a paw.

"Finally Ben cornered Fu Fu at the back of the yard. He kept trying to pet her and pick her up. I told him to stop. I tried to get him to play with me, instead. I tried to warn him, but . . ." I took a deep breath, sighed. "But he didn't understand. When he tried to pick Fu Fu up, she bit his hand. He jumped back, and Fu Fu bit him on the leg.

When Ben ran away, she chased him. She kept biting at him, and she got ahold of his leg again.

"That made me mad. I mean, she'd already chased him away. He was crying and hurt, but she just kept snapping and snarling and biting. I ran after them. I told her to leave my Ben alone, but she bit him again. He fell down and started crying really loud. I had to make her stop! I couldn't let her hurt my little boy. So . . . so . . . I bit her.

"I didn't mean to bite her hard. I just wanted to make her stop hurting my boy. But . . . well, she was little and I was big. When I picked her up, Fu Fu screamed. I threw her across the yard. She didn't get up, at first. She just whined and squirmed around on the ground.

"Fu Fu finally got to her feet, but she could barely walk. She limped and cried as if I'd half killed her. I didn't mean to bite her. I didn't think I had really hurt her. I just wanted to get her away from my boy. But I was mad and . . . and . . . my Ben was still crying, and a little blood leaked from a hole on his leg where Fu Fu had nipped him. I nuzzled him with my nose. I kissed him with my tongue, but he kept crying. I was afraid he might be really hurt, so I picked him up and took him to the house, and . . . and then . . ."

I couldn't finish. I was shaking all over.

"Let me guess," Red snorted. "Ben's father came out to see what all the crying was about. He saw Fu Fu lying in the yard and saw his boy dangling from your mouth."

I nodded, feeling my tail begin to tuck itself under my tummy.

"When you tried to explain that you'd saved your boy from Fu Fu, the father wouldn't listen, right?"

I nodded again and flattened my ears against my head. "I guess he thought I had attacked Fu Fu, then turned on Ben. I guess he didn't know I was bringing Ben to his daddy. He must have thought I had bitten Ben, too.

"I'd never bite my boy. I loved him. I'd never do anything to hurt him. But that's when I smelled it—the fear. I'd never smelled it before—that was the first time. It was a little different from the smell of that burglar and the smell from the coyotes, but very close. The smell jumped from the daddy so strong that I could taste it, even with Ben in my mouth. He took Ben away from me and kicked me. Right on the side of my head. That spot still hurts. I can feel it now, just as if it happened yesterday instead of a long time ago."

I flopped down on the ground and covered my

face with my ears and paws. I felt so rotten and sad that I almost made myself sick. My tail was tucked under me so tightly that I couldn't even feel it. My nose, which was always cold and damp, felt as hot and dry as a bone that had been left in the sun. I wanted to curl up and die.

Chapter 10

Poky and Red tried to comfort me. They nuzzled me with their noses. They licked my ears and nudged me with their paws. They talked to me and rubbed their cheeks against my forehead.

"You did the right thing," Red told me. "The poodle was hurting your boy. You had to make her stop."

"I didn't mean to hurt her," I sniffed. "She never could walk very well after that. They had to take her to the vet and . . . and . . . after she came home, she still limped." I sighed and let my ears droop over my eyes. "Fu Fu always limped."

"It wasn't your fault," Poky whispered in my ear. "Fu Fu's limp wasn't your fault, and the daddy getting scared wasn't your fault, either. He shouldn't have kicked you."

"Why couldn't I make him understand?" I whined.

Red grunted when he stumbled to his feet. "People can't understand dip," he snorted. "I heard that they *could* understand a long, long time ago. Then they learned this thing they call language—you know, the words they use. Ever since they got words, that's the only way they can talk. We use wiggles of our ears and our tails. We smell, we taste, we look. They forgot how to smell and taste and look. If they can't talk with words, they can't understand a stinking thing. I tried to tell my master about the coyotes. Idiot just looked at me and patted my head. You can wiggle your ears and give off your smells and twitch your hair till you're blue in the face. Without words, people can't understand diddly-squat."

Poky stood up and looked toward the back fence. It was getting late. "What *are* we going to do about the coyotes?"

My tail didn't wag, but at least I could feel it again. Red shoved me hard with his snout. I got to my feet. My nose was still hot and my insides shook, but I took a deep breath and cocked my ears away from my head so I could hear Red.

"Sweetie," he said. His eyes and ears spoke

very seriously. "You're going to have to do something. Poky is too little, and I'm too old. You're going to have to fight the coyotes. We can help, but we can't do it without you."

I shook my head. My ears popped against my cheeks. "I can't fight. I can't bite!"

"Why?" Red snarled. "Because you made a mistake once and bit some old lady on the bottom?"

"No. Because of what I did to Fu Fu and to Ben."

"You didn't do anything to your Ben. You helped him, and the dumb daddy just didn't understand."

"But what about Fu Fu?"

"She deserved it."

"Oh, no." I cringed. "She didn't deserve to limp for the rest of her life."

Red put one paw over the other and squinted at me. "You might not have even hurt her. She sounds like the kind of dog who just might be faking her limp to make the mama feel sorry for her and not throw her outside when she messes on the floor. Even if you really did hurt her, which I doubt, you didn't mean to. What would have happened if you hadn't done something?"

I shrugged my ear.

"What would have happened?" he repeated.

"Well, I guess she would have kept biting my boy."

"Right."

"She would have kept hurting him."

Red gave a knowing nod. "You did what you had to do to protect your master. You're still hung up about your brothers and sisters calling you a bully. You don't growl or bite because you're big and you figure you might hurt somebody. But if you hadn't stopped Fu Fu, she would have hurt Ben even worse. When you fight to protect your master, you're not being a bully. You have to do what's right."

Red grunted as he got to his feet. He stood in front of me—so close that his nose touched mine.

"You're scared that you might get sent to the pound. But even if it's dangerous—even if your people might not understand—you still have to do what's right. Doing the right thing isn't easy, sometimes. But if you don't do anything, if you just think being a good watchdog means doing nothing but sitting and watching . . . well, you still got in trouble with your master, remember. It's much better to do what's right, even if you get in trouble, than to do nothing at all.

"You have to help Poky and me with the coyotes. Protecting your friends isn't nearly as important as protecting your master, but we need you. We can't do it alone."

Red's words made sense. He took his nose away from mine and sat down. When he did, he groaned again. Red was old and feeble because of his arthritis, but he was wise. Very wise. Still . . .

I plopped down on my bottom and crunched my tail again. I didn't even move it, though. I just sat on it.

"I'm so confused," I confessed. "When I was a puppy, I was confused all the time. But I thought that when I grew up I'd know things. I wouldn't be confused. Only . . . now I'm grown up, and I still don't know . . ."

"What are you confused about?" Poky asked with a wag of his tail.

"Well . . ." I felt my cheeks puff out when I sighed. "When I smelled fear on the burglar, I should have chased him off. Right?"

"Right."

"And when I smelled fear on the coyotes, I should have bitten them, right?"

"Right."

"But I smelled fear on Ben's daddy and on my friend Scotty when he was headed for the pound, and I smell it on Red when he thinks about the coyotes. Am I supposed to bite them, too?"

Red stood up again. "No. It's a different smell.

Different kinds of fear have separate smells. They're very close, but different. One odor is simple. Your Ben's father was afraid you had hurt his boy or would hurt him. Scotty was afraid of the pound, and I'm afraid of the coyotes.

"The other smell—the one from the burglar and the coyotes—their smell is because they're scared of getting caught doing something they're not supposed to. The burglar knows it's wrong to steal, and the coyotes know it's wrong to take our food. It's still a fear smell, but it's sort of a sneaky smell, too. It's hard for people and animals to be brave when they know they're doing something that's not right."

I nodded, remembering how the smells were the same, only different. "Why does the smell of fear hurt my nose and at the same time make me feel big and strong inside?"

"A long, long time ago, before we befriended people, we dogs had to take care of ourselves," Red explained. "There were animals we could eat and animals that would eat us. All fear smelled the same back then. Life was much simpler. When we ran across something that smelled of fear, our bodies told us to chase it so we could eat. That's where the strong feeling comes from. But when people came . . . well, we like people, and we don't want to eat them. But sometimes they smell of fear, too. Most of us have learned to overcome our instincts and not chase them."

"I think I understand now." I smiled. "One kind of fear—when people are afraid of us because they don't know us or because we're big—we leave them alone. The other kind of fear—the sneaky kind—that's when we chase and bite."

Red's white hair at the side of his mouth curled to a smile. "Right."

Poky's brown eyes opened wide. "Then you'll help us with the coyotes?"

"Yes."

The coyotes didn't come when they usually did. I guess it was because Poky's master worked outside in the yard until after dark. He was piling hay and straw around his roses and cactuses because of the cold.

I ate every bit of my food. It felt good to have a full tummy. As soon as Poky's master went inside, Poky and Red came to my yard. It was cold, but we were full and cozy. We curled up in the spot at the middle of my yard where we had been sleeping. I don't know why we didn't go into my house. I guess we were just used to the low spot in my yard.

It was a lot easier to sleep, now that my belly was full and now that I wasn't confused anymore.

WATCHDOG AND THE COYOTES

How long I slept I didn't know. But in the very middle of the night Poky lifted my ear with his nose.

"I think we're in big trouble," Poky whispered. With his paw he nudged Red. "Wake up, Red. This looks really bad!"

Chapter 11

*T*here were twelve coyotes in my yard. While we slept, they had formed a circle around us. When Poky woke me, I saw the coyotes watching us with their yellow eyes. They licked their lips.

"We're hungry!" The leader drooled.

Still half asleep, I struggled to my feet. Our tummies were full, but we were still cold and weak from hunger. "We have no more food," I said. "You've eaten it all."

"So?" one scoffed. "You guys look pretty tasty to us."

"Yeah," another added. "I bet that little one there—the one with the big ears and long tail—I bet he's downright yummy."

They all laughed. It was an evil-sounding laugh. Yellow eyes shining, white fangs glowing in the night, they took a step closer.

"Get 'em, Sweetie!" Poky whispered.

I leaned close to his floppy ear. "Let's try, just once more, to be friends."

Poky rolled his soft brown eyes.

I turned to face the coyotes. "If you eat us," I reasoned, "there will be no more food. Without us, our masters will quit filling the bowls. Then you will have nothing. Nothing at all."

"We're hungry, now."

The circle of coyotes tightened.

"That big one ought to feed six or seven of us," one coyote yapped.

"I want a leg," another chuckled.

"I want his guts," yapped another.

I took a deep breath. I didn't want to bite. But I was not a coward. I took a brave step toward the coyotes. "Take me," I said, "but please don't eat my friends."

The big coyote, who always seemed to do most of the talking, grinned. "That's what we're planning to do."

"Yeah," another coyote snickered. "And when we get through with you, we'll eat those other scrawny mutts, too."

They all laughed and took another step closer.

Red backed his rump against me. He bared his teeth and growled. "There are some animals you just can't reason with. We've either got to fight or die."

Poky leaned against my leg from the other direction. "Ready to get 'em, Sweetie?"

"I'm ready," I whispered.

I felt the hair ridge-up along my back. I bared my teeth. Growled.

Only it had been so long since I'd growled that just a little "fruff" came out.

I took a deep breath so I could bark at the mean coyotes.

Only it had been so long since I'd barked that all I said was "yap."

The coyotes howled and laughed. One jumped in and nipped me on the leg. It hurt. I tried to bite him back. Only it had been so long since I'd bitten, my jaws didn't open. My cheeks just puffed in and out, making a little popping sound.

The leader of the coyotes jumped on Red. The Irish setter fought bravely, but in no time at all, two other coyotes had helped the leader knock him down. One chomped down hard on Red's leg.

Poky fought and snapped, but he wasn't very big. Two coyotes grabbed him. One holding each of Poky's hind legs, they stretched him out and started dragging him off across the yard.

Five pounced on me. Their sharp teeth hurt. I growled, but it was a soft, weak sound. I bit, but my jaws were so gentle that my teeth wouldn't have hurt a kitten. All I could do was stand there as they bit and slashed at me with their glistening white fangs.

I screamed with the pain. I hoped and prayed it would be over soon.

Chapter 12

Light flooded the yard.

"What's all the racket? Get out of here!" My master screamed as he threw open the back door. "Get away from there, you stinkin' coyotes."

In a blink of an eye, the coyotes scattered. A couple ran for the holes on either side of the yard. Most jumped the back fence and went slinking off into the desert.

As the three of us lay panting and whimpering in the yard, my master went back inside and got a flashlight. I could tell that he wondered what Poky and Red were doing in my yard. He didn't ask. Instead, when he came out again, he checked to see how bad our injuries were. Poky, Red, and

I each licked his hand and thanked him for saving our lives.

We were bleeding and hurt, but our wounds were not serious. My master went back inside his house. Poky, Red, and I huddled in my big doghouse and licked our wounds.

"They'll be back," Poky said. "We don't stand a chance."

I licked the cut on my paw. "We *do* stand a chance," I assured my friend. "My master scared them. He will watch to make sure they don't come back."

Red sniffed. He had a big cut on his nose where one of the coyotes had sunk his fangs in. "He won't watch forever. When the coyotes think it's safe, and when your master's no longer watching for them, they'll come back. Next time there may be even more coyotes. Your master may not always be here to protect us."

I licked my paw again. "Then we must learn to protect ourselves," I said. "It's been so long since I have barked or bitten that I've forgotten how. Tomorrow we go into training."

"What's training?" Poky whimpered as he tried to lick the cut on his neck.

"We're gonna get in shape. My first master in California used to run and lift weights and do exercises. It was to make him look pretty for the big little girls, but it also made him stronger. That's what we're going to do."

Before our masters woke in the morning, Red and Poky went back to their yards. They dug two new holes, right in the center of the yard by the fence. Sure enough, when my master told their masters about Red and Poky being in my yard last night, they came to investigate.

Since the new holes were in plain sight, they used shovels to put the dirt back. They never bothered to look for the other hole on Red's side of the fence or the broken boards at the back of Poky's yard.

As soon as they left, I started our training.

Since the coyotes had stolen all our bones, I sent Poky for supplies. His master's son had left a softball, a bat, and a basketball in the yard.

Poky's hind legs were stiff because the coyotes had tried to make a wishbone out of him, but he brought the things back to my yard.

Red and I took turns biting and gnawing on the baseball bat. Poky chewed the softball. Picking it up in his mouth, he would bite down as hard as he could. Then he would shake it and throw it high in the air. The second it landed, he would chase after it and bite it again.

I chased the basketball. I tried to bite it, but it

was just a little too big for me to get my mouth around. I chased it, nonetheless. I tried to pin it against the corner of the fence, and if it got away from me, I chased it some more.

Each night we slept in my doghouse. Each evening, before bed, we practiced our growling and snarling. We took turns snapping at each other, too. We wouldn't snap hard, but it was good practice at moving our nose or paw before it got bitten.

At first light we tumbled out of the doghouse. We ran twenty laps, one behind the other, around my big backyard. After biting practice, we played chase.

Red grumped and complained about his arthritis. He didn't like all the running, but he knew he needed to get in shape. With each day that passed, he could run longer and farther before he got tired.

Poky wasn't as fast as Red and I were. He was quick, though. Just as one of us would close in on him during the chase game, he would dodge to the side or double back. My big, long legs carried me so fast that once I stepped on him. Gamely, the beagle jumped up and shook himself. Then he and Red chased me.

A week passed, and no coyotes.

All three of us felt much better. Without the

coyotes, there was plenty of food. Our tummies were full. Our wounds had healed. We felt stronger with the passing of each day.

Then, late one night, the coyotes howled in the desert.

Poky trembled. He scooted closer against my side in my doghouse. "I knew they'd be back."

Red raised his head. "Maybe we should go out and bark at them. We could tell them how strong we are now. We could warn them not to come back. If we do that, maybe they won't bother us."

I didn't answer him. My tail made a thumping sound on the floor of my doghouse.

"They are way off in the desert," Poky said, still shoving himself against my side. "They probably won't come until tomorrow night."

The next day, it was training as usual. Red didn't grump about running laps. Poky bit the ball harder than he ever had before. I chased the big basketball around and around and around. If I could just . . .

Blamb!

Poky and Red were getting a drink. Both wheeled around.

With a smug grin on my face, I came trotting

83

toward them. A limp, flat basketball hung from my mouth. I dropped it at my friends' feet.

"I think we're ready," I said.

That night the coyotes howled again. My master and his wife drove away in their car. Where they went, I didn't know. I did know there was no one to keep watch. There was no one to turn on the light. There was no one to protect us but *us.*

A little after dark we heard the coyotes jump over the fence into Poky's yard. They laughed and burped as they ate his food.

"Shouldn't we go get 'em?" Poky asked.

I didn't answer.

A nose poked through the broken boards in the fence. The coyote sneered and looked around. I lay in the opening of my doghouse, resting my chin on my paws. The coyote disappeared, and we could hear them jumping the back fence into Red's yard.

When I heard them munching on the table scraps and the bones, I turned to Red. "Now," I whispered.

Red climbed over me and raced across the yard. He hid in the dark behind one of the shrubs. I turned to Poky.

"Now."

Poky started to climb over me, but then he stopped. "You're not going to try to reason with them again, are you? You do remember how to bite?"

I smiled. *"Now,"* I repeated.

Poky trotted quietly across the yard and hid in the dark by his fence.

After a while, when the coyotes were through joking and laughing and burping and slobbering, one appeared at the hole under the fence.

He saw me lying in the doghouse. He sneered and slipped through the fence. Another followed.

One, two, three, four, five, six, seven . . . Twelve coyotes slipped through the opening.

I crawled out of my doghouse. The coyotes came up and formed a circle around me.

"Where are your buddies?" The big leader licked his lips.

I didn't answer.

"It don't matter," he scoffed. "We'll just eat this one first. Then we can find the other two. They're probably hiding in the doghouse."

I forced the ridge of hair on my back to stay down. I didn't let my lip curl or my white teeth show.

"Wouldn't you rather be friends, Mr. Coyote?"

All the coyotes laughed and yapped. "Sure," one said. "We'll be friends."

"Yeah," another added, "just as soon as we're through eating you, we'll be the best of friends."

The big coyote trotted right up in my face. He snarled at me and showed his long fangs. "Why don't you just lie down, big boy? Make it a little easier on us." His nose was almost touching mine.

"Well, Mr. Coyote," I said softly. "If you don't want to be friends. Then . . ."

The big coyote's eyes flashed wide. All he could see was the empty cavern of my throat when I opened my mouth. I bit down as hard as I could.

The coyote's whole head was inside my huge jaws. When I let go, the coyote fell backwards. He tumbled over himself a couple of times. He landed on his back with his feet flopping in the air. Dazed, he finally managed to crawl to his feet.

His eyes rolled around in his face. He shook his head. Slobbers went flying all over the other coyotes.

"Did you see that?" he gasped. "He almost bit my head off." His eyes rolled again. "Man, talk about a headache!"

I took a deep breath and in my loudest roar I screamed:

"Charge!"

Chapter 13

Before the other coyotes knew what was happening, I flew into them. Poky and Red charged, growling and snarling, out of the dark shadows at the corners of my yard.

Red knocked one coyote down. The coyote rolled about three times from the force of Red's powerful legs. Then Red bit another coyote on the back. Poky leaped at the coyote nearest him. Poky was small, but he did give the coyote a terrible bite, right on his soft tummy. The coyote squalled and fell over on his side.

With my mighty jaws I bit one, then another. With my big paws, I clunked a coyote on top of the head. I hit him with such force that the coyote fell spread-eagled to the ground and bumped his chin in the dirt.

A coyote lunged for Poky. Just as he had practiced in the chase game, Poky dodged out of the way. Before the coyote could turn, the beagle circled around behind him and chomped down on the coyote's leg. Squealing at the top of his lungs, the coyote raced across the yard, dragging Poky behind him.

One coyote jumped the fence. Then another and another.

Red chased one, snapping at his rump every step of the way. The coyote tried to jump the fence. But he was trying so hard to get away from Red's fierce jaws that he jumped a bit too soon. He didn't quite make it.

There was a loud crack as the coyote's head slammed into the fence. It broke a chunk of wood out. The coyote bounced off the fence and went flying backwards over Red. Before he could scramble to his feet, the Irish setter bit him once on the ear and once, really hard, on the nose. Running for his life, the coyote had to circle the yard again before he could get up enough speed to jump the fence. He made it this time. But he was in such a hurry that he scraped his tummy on the fence and left a whole bunch of hair stuck to the boards.

Through the broken-off chunk in the fence, I could see him. Tail tucked between his legs, he slinked off into the desert.

Suddenly all was quiet.

Red turned to help his friends. Poky was nowhere in sight and I didn't need any help.

Only one coyote was left—the big one who usually did all the talking. He lay in the middle of the yard. I stood over him, smiling. With my big paws, I pinned him to the ground.

"Please let me up," the coyote whined. "Please don't hurt me. Please let me go."

I ignored him. When Red came trotting over, I winked. "What do you think we should do with this coyote?"

Red winked back at me.

"Let's eat him for supper."

The coyote whimpered. Terrified, he kicked his feet and struggled to get up. It took hardly any effort at all for me to hold him down. The smell of his fear was so strong that it burned my nose. It almost made my eyes water.

Suddenly I began to wonder why Poky wasn't with us. I looked around. A bit nervous, scared that something bad might have happened to my friend, I was just about to let go of the coyote and search for Poky when another coyote shot through the broken boards on Poky's side of the fence.

"Would you look at him?" I told Red.

The coyote raced across the yard. He whimpered and yapped and squalled every step of the way. And there, behind him, was Poky—still holding on to his hind leg and flopping like a flag waving in the breeze.

The coyote shot through the hole into Red's yard.

"Poky," I called, "let go of that coyote and come over here."

Poky didn't answer. In a moment or two the coyote shot back through the hole under the fence, headed in the other direction. The beagle still clung to his leg as he crawled through the boards into Poky's yard.

"Poky," Red called, "let go of him and come here."

Again there was no answer.

Yapping and screaming and crying, the coyote—with the beagle still hanging on to his leg—raced back and forth between the two holes in the fence about five times.

Finally Red turned to me.

"Reckon I should go get him?"

I shrugged my ears. "Guess so. If you don't,

he'll keep chewing on that poor coyote's leg all night."

The big coyote—the one that I was holding down—tried to slip free. I bopped him on the head with my paw.

"Be still!"

Red trotted to the hole in Poky's fence. This time, as the coyote came slipping through, Red leaned down and caught ahold of Poky's tail.

"Let go of me!" Poky growled. "I'm gonna chew this guy's leg off."

It was a bit hard to understand him because he had a mouthful of coyote leg.

Red didn't let go. He held on to Poky's tail. The coyote stopped. With Poky hanging on to his leg and Red hanging on to Poky, the coyote tried to run, but he couldn't. He kept jerking and struggling to get away.

It reminded me of a tug-of-war game. Red on one side, the coyote on the other. And Poky was the rope. The beagle was stretched out between the two bigger animals. His feet dangled about six inches off the ground.

"Let go, Poky!" Red growled. "He's had enough."

It was a bit hard to understand Red because he had a mouthful of beagle tail.

Finally, Poky released his grip. Still crying, the

coyote limped for the back of the yard. His leg must have really hurt, because it took him three jumps before he finally got over the fence. Then he whimpered and limped off into the darkness.

Red licked Poky right on top of the head. "Good job. You really showed him."

"Yeah, I did."

With his head held high on one end and his tail sticking up high on the other, Poky came prancing across the yard.

All three of us glared down at the large coyote—the one with the big mouth.

"What are we gonna do with this one?" Poky asked.

"I don't know," I answered.

"I think we should eat him." Red winked again.

The big coyote struggled, helpless to get up. "Oh, please, please," he begged. "Don't eat me."

"You ate all our food," Poky growled. "Now we don't have anything to eat for supper. We'll *have* to eat you."

Red tilted his head to the side. He sniffed. "I don't know," he said thoughtfully. "If he tastes half as bad as he smells, he would probably make us sick." He made a snorting sound and wrinkled his nose.

"He's right!" the coyote pleaded. "I *do* stink.

Besides that, I'm tough and stringy. You guys wouldn't like me at all."

I smiled at my friends. "I think Poky is right. Even if this coyote does stink, and even if he is a little tough, let's eat him. I'll hold him down and you guys go ahead. After all, it was your food that he ate."

The big coyote cried and whined and wiggled. "Wait," he begged. "Let's talk this over. Let's be friends."

"Oh," I snarled. "So *now* you want to be friends?"

The big coyote whimpered and cried and squalled. We looked down at him. We couldn't keep from sneering at the coward.

Finally I leaned over and picked him up by the tail. He dangled, limply from my mouth. I was so tall that he didn't even touch the ground when I trotted across the yard.

At the back fence I stopped. I aimed with my left eye. With one jerk of my head, I flung the coyote skyward.

He went sailing high up in the air. His feet churned. His tail spun.

Suddenly I realized that was his rear spinning, not his tail. My eyes crossed as I looked down my snout. His tail still dangled from my mouth.

"Oops," I mumbled. "Musta forgot to let go."

The coyote flew so high into the sky that he almost seemed to touch the silver-white moon. Then he came crashing down.

There was a loud *clank* from the other side of the fence. We moved closer and peeked through the cracks between the boards. The big coyote had landed in a trash can. There was more clanking and rattling as the coyote struggled to get out. The trash can finally tipped over. Covered with lettuce, sour milk, used tissues, and all sorts of stinky, yucky stuff, the big coyote came crawling out.

If he'd had his tail, he would have tucked it under him. As it was, he tucked his bottom and went slinking off into the desert. I knew we'd never see the coyotes, ever again.

Chapter 14

Red was a little sore and stiff for a couple of days. Poky went around coughing and spitting and complaining about how bad coyotes tasted. I couldn't help but notice the little twinkle in his eye each time he griped about it, though.

For the next three weeks life was calm and peaceful. We played together when our masters were at work. At night we either slept together in my big doghouse or enjoyed the peace and quiet of sleeping alone in our own yards.

Then one afternoon I heard a rattling sound at my back gate. The hair bristled in a sharp ridge down my back. My muscles tightened.

I watched.

A man opened the gate and peeked in. He wore a black stocking cap. Without a sound I eased to my feet. I had to lean down to see out of my doghouse because I was so tall that my head almost touched the ceiling. The man shut the gate behind him and started across my yard. Then his eyes fell on my huge house. He must have seen me watching. Suddenly he froze. He didn't move, he didn't tremble, he didn't even breathe.

I eased through the doorway and walked on stiff legs toward him.

As I neared, he held out one hand, offering his knuckles for me to sniff. Although he wore a black cap like the burglar, he was not the same man. His face was different, and his smell was not the same as that of the thief who had come in the night.

"Nice dog." His voice quavered. "Nice dog. Hope you're a good dog."

The smell of fear was strong. It hurt my nose, but at the same time it made me feel big and strong inside. I followed him as he eased his way to the back of my master's house. There he moved a bush aside with the back of his hand and looked down at something.

I watched.

"I'm just reading the electric meter," he assured me, looking down at a glass thing that stuck up from some pipes at the back of the house. "Nice dog. I'm not going to bother anything. Good puppy."

He took a sharp pointed thing from his pocket and scratched on a pad. Then he let go of the bush and moved slowly away.

I watched.

But I didn't follow him. His smell of fear was simply a smell of fear. There was no sneaky taste to it. There was nothing sly or evil about the way he moved. He slipped through the gate at the back of my fence and closed it behind him.

Poky came over that afternoon. He was excited and happy because his master had finally gotten him a new chewy bone. When Red crawled through the hole from his side of the fence, Poky offered to share his chewy bone with us.

He was so proud of his new bone that Red and I just didn't have the heart to get slobbers all over it. We decided to at least let Poky chew the new off his bone before we shared it.

It was early spring when trouble came to visit. It came at night, just as it had before. I lay in my doghouse with my paws folded, resting my chin on them where they draped over the edge of my floor.

There was a sound at the back fence. My ears perked.

I watched.

A black stocking cap appeared at the top of my fence. There was a *clunk* as a man's foot found the bottom rail. He climbed over the fence.

I watched.

The man was dressed in black. His shirt was black, and he wore black pants and black gloves. For a moment he hesitated and looked around.

I watched.

Boldly he walked across the yard, straight to my doghouse.

"Hi, you dumb mutt." He smiled. "You remember me? I remember you. You're the same dog who was here last time I broke into this place."

The smell of fear came from him. It was not the simple smell of fear. This was the same sly, sneaky smell that had come from this man when he stole things from my master's house. It was the same sneaky smell that had come from the coyotes when they stole our food. It was the smell of fear that came when someone did something they knew was wrong and they were afraid they might get caught.

I felt the hair stand on end along my back. I eased to my feet.

"I may look like the same dog," I said. "But I'm not. You'd better get out of my master's yard."

But I guess people just don't understand Dog.

The man walked to the back door and started jiggling the doorknob. I walked right up behind him.

"Figure it's been long enough since I was here last for the folks inside to collect their insurance money and buy all new stuff." The man's voice was as sneaky as his smell.

"I warned you," I growled. "You'd better leave. You'd better not rob my master's house again."

He gave me a funny look when I growled at him, but even with my second warning, I guess he still didn't understand. "Beat it, mutt," he said. "I'm busy. Bet the guy's got a new VCR and TV and new everything." He took a long bar from a black bag that he carried. He pushed it into the side of the door and started to pry it open.

I shrugged my ears. "All right. I tried to warn you."

Red and blue lights flashed. Weird, funny shadows danced across my yard. A tall, lean man in a blue uniform stood beside my master. He scratched his head and looked at me. I smiled back. Then he turned to my master.

"I can't quite figure it out, Mr. Shaffer," the

man said. "Your neighbors called us. They reported hearing screams, like someone was being killed. Before you got home, we checked the premises. There's a mark on your back door, as if someone tried to break in with a crowbar or something. And we found a pant leg from a pair of black slacks hanging on your back fence. But that's all we found."

Mr. Shaffer looked at me and scratched his head. "Officer, may I borrow your flashlight for a moment?"

The policeman handed Mr. Shaffer his light and followed him to my doghouse. My master dropped to one knee and shone his light inside. In the back corner of my house were my trophies—my reminders that I wasn't really a bully if I fought to protect myself or my friends.

"See anything?" The policeman leaned down next to him.

Mr. Shaffer almost laughed. "Not much. Just a coyote tail, a crowbar, and a black stocking cap."

The policeman chuckled as he got to his feet. "Looks like an attempted burglary. Your dog must have run the thief off before he could get into the house. Looks like you got yourself one heck of a watchdog there, Mr. Shaffer."

My master grunted as he got to his feet. He

handed the officer his flashlight, then came over and started patting my head.

"Best watchdog a man could ever want," he bragged. "Sweetie, you're some watchdog."

This time, when my master said the word "watchdog," that was exactly what he meant. I felt so big and proud I could have popped. My tail began to wag. It almost knocked the policeman down. It pounded against the side of my doghouse like someone beating on a bass drum.

"You're some watchdog." My master's words drummed in my ears even louder than my tail drummed against my doghouse. Those were the words I had always wanted to hear more than anything else in the world.

"Watchdog."

The word made my chest fill with pride. My tail wagged harder. Suddenly my whole back end was wagging. Then my middle and even my shoulders wagged. I wasn't wagging my tail—my tail was wagging me. Even my ears began to flop. Finally I was a watchdog.

About the Author

BILL WALLACE was a principal and physical education teacher for ten years at the same elementary school he attended as a child in his hometown of Chickasha, Oklahoma. A family who enjoys the outdoors, the Wallaces spend much of their spare time fishing, quail hunting, or tending cattle on the family farm. Bill helps his wife and son care for their four dogs, three cats, and two horses, lectures at schools around the country, answers mail from his readers, and, of course, works on his books. His novels have won sixteen state awards and made the master lists in twenty-four states.